WALT DISNEY PRODUCTIONS
presents

Aladdin and his

Book Club Edition

Wonderful Lamp

Random House New York

First American Edition
Copyright © 1978 by The Walt Disney Company. All rights reserved under International and Pan-American
Copyright Conventions. Published in the United States by Random House, Inc., New York, and simulta-
neously in Canada by Random House of Canada Limited, Toronto. Originally published in Denmark as
Aladdin og den vidunderlige lampe by Gutenberghus Bladene, Copenhagen. ISBN: 0-394-83937-4 ISBN:
0-394-93937-9 (library bdg.)

Manufactured in the United States of America
DEFGHIJK   7 8 9 0

Aladdin and his mother lived
long ago in a town far, far away.
They were very poor.

Every day Aladdin went to the market place to find work. But there were never any jobs for someone his size.

Then one day a stranger said: "Would you like to earn a gold piece?"

Aladdin was very excited.
One gold piece could buy so much!
"I have a job for someone just your
size," said the stranger. "Follow me."

The man led Aladdin out of town.
They went along for many miles.

When they came to a mountain,
the man stopped.

"Make a small fire right here,"
he told Aladdin.

Aladdin was puzzled.
What did the stranger plan to do?

Aladdin picked up
some sticks.

He made a small fire.
While the fire burned,
the man began to say
many strange words—
words that Aladdin
did not understand.

Suddenly a piece of the mountain
began to open—like a door.
Behind this door there was a hole.
The hole was just big enough
for someone Aladdin's size.

"Inside you will find
an old lamp," said the man.
"Bring it to me."

"G-g-go in there?" asked Aladdin.
"Yes, yes, of course," said the man.
"That hole is the only entrance. Now
hurry! It does not stay open for long."

The stranger watched as Aladdin
crept down some narrow steps.

"Don't stop to take anything but
the lamp!" he called.

The steps led to a great room
filled with gold pieces.

Aladdin wanted to fill his pockets
but he did not stop.

He knew he must hurry.

The next room
was even bigger.
In this room
there was a tree.
On the tree
there were jewels.

The jewels looked
just like fruit!

Under the jewel
tree lay an old lamp.

Aladdin picked up the old lamp
and started to go.

Then he thought:

"No one will mind if I take
a few jewels to show my mother."

And so he did.

Suddenly he heard the stranger
calling to him:
"Come back! The hole will close."
Aladdin turned and ran.

He came to the narrow steps.

"Faster! Faster!" cried the man.

But Aladdin could not make his feet
go any faster.

"Throw me the lamp!" said the man.
"I must have that lamp."

"I will bring it,"
called Aladdin.

"There is no time,"
said the man. "The hole
is going to close."

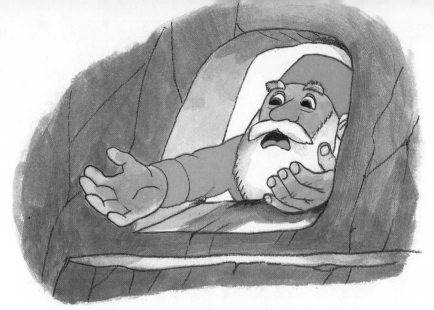

The stranger held out his arms.
"The lamp! The lamp!" he cried.

The hole in the mountain
grew smaller and smaller.
Then it disappeared.

Aladdin was trapped inside the mountain.

"All because of this silly old lamp!"

he thought.

Aladdin rubbed the old lamp sadly.

At once there
was a great puff
of smoke.
SWOOSH!
Out of the lamp
popped a genie!

"What is your wish,
O Master of the Lamp?"
asked the genie.

"My wish!"
said Aladdin.
"That's simple.
I wish I were
home."

Before he knew what had
happened, Aladdin was back
at his house.

His mother was glad to see him.

And she was amazed to hear his story.

"But how sad!" she said. "All those riches and here we are, as poor as ever. Maybe we can sell the lamp if I polish it."

She took a cloth and began to rub the lamp.

At once there
was a great puff
of smoke.
SWOOSH!
Out of the
lamp popped the
genie.

'Your wish
O Master?"
he asked.

"I wish we could have some supper,"
said Aladdin. "I'm hungry."

At once a feast appeared on silver dishes.

After they ate, Aladdin's
mother put away the silver dishes.

One by one Aladdin took the dishes
to the market place to sell.

This way Aladdin
and his mother were
able to buy all the
things they needed.

One day Aladdin
went off to sell
the last dish.

On his way he saw
the Sultan's daughter.
She was riding in a
sedan chair.

The princess smiled at him.
Aladdin had never been so happy.
He dropped the silver dish
and ran after the sedan chair.
"I must talk to her,"
he thought.

Aladdin followed the sedan chair
to the Sultan's palace.

Two palace guards were standing
by the door.

"I want to see the princess,"
Aladdin told them.

"A poor lad to see
the princess!" said the
guard.
"Send him to me,"
said the Sultan.

Aladdin was led into the palace.
There sat the Sultan himself.
"I have come to see the princess,"
said Aladdin.

"If you want
to see her, you
must bring me
a present,"
said the Sultan.

"I have something right here,"
said Aladdin.

He gave him the jewels
from the cave.

"Perfect!" said the Sultan.
"Now go put on your finest clothes
and you may see the princess."

Aladdin walked home sadly.

He looked for one more silver dish.

He could sell it and buy new clothes.

But all
the silver
dishes were
gone.

But there was
e wonderful lamp!

As soon as
laddin rubbed it,
e genie appeared.

Aladdin asked him
for some
fine clothes.

Quicker than quick, Aladdin found himself
dressed like a prince in the middle of a palace.

The Sultan and his daughter were coming down
a long walk.

Aladdin bowed to the Sultan.

"My name is Aladdin," he said.
"I am here to see the princess."

The princess
laughed.

"I saw you
in the market
place," she said.

"Come now, Princess," said the Sultan.
"This is nobody from town. This is a prince.
We must welcome him into our home."

Soon Aladdin and the princess were married.
Now Aladdin was rich and
important and happy.
He never needed the genie again.